BIG, SCARY WOLF

Written and illustrated by
HARVEY STEVENSON

CLARION BOOKS
New York

Clarion Books
a Houghton Mifflin Company imprint
215 Park Avenue South, New York, NY 10003
Text and illustrations copyright © 1997 by Harvey Stevenson

The illustrations for this book were executed in acrylic paints on paper.
The text is set in 18/24-point Dante medium.

For information about this and other Houghton Mifflin
trade and reference books and multimedia products,
visit The Bookstore at Houghton Mifflin on the World Wide Web
at (http://www.hmco.com/trade/).

Printed in Singapore

Library of Congress Cataloging-in-Publication Data

Stevenson, Harvey.
Big, scary wolf / written and illustrated by Harvey Stevenson.
p.   cm.
Summary: Rose is too scared to sleep at night
because she knows there's a big, scary wolf in her room,
so she tells Papa about it and he helps her dispel her fears.
ISBN 0-395-74213-7
[1. Wolves—Fiction.   2. Fear—Fiction.   3. Night—Fiction.]   I. Title.
PZ7.S84745Bi   1997
[E]—dc20   95-26334
CIP
AC

TWP   10 9 8 7 6 5 4 3 2 1

For Rose, with love.

Rose couldn't sleep. She lay in bed with
her eyes open.
   The shadows in her room seemed to move.
   She pulled up her blankets and stared
into the darkness.

Swish, swish, whispered the night wind outside.
Click, click, went the shadows on the floor.
"A furry tail . . . long claws . . . a scary wolf!"
thought Rose, trying to be very still.

Something went *drip, drip, drip*.
"A *hungry* scary wolf!" thought Rose.
She looked at the door.
"How fast can a wolf run after a little girl?"
she wondered.

Rose held her breath, jumped from her bed,
and ran into her parents' room.

"What is it, Rose?" asked Papa.

"There's a big, mean, scary wolf in my room!"
cried Rose. "I saw him!"

11

"Now what would a wolf be doing in your room?"
asked Papa. "Did you invite him in?"
"Of course not," said Rose.

"Well, I didn't either," said Papa.
"Maybe he's lost."
"Maybe," said Rose.

13

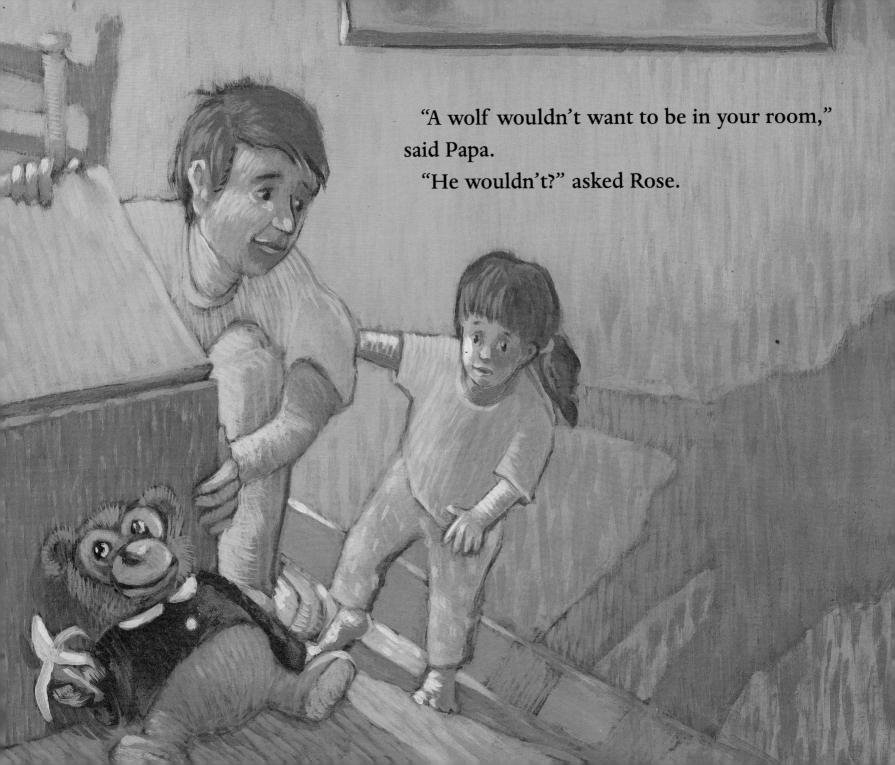

"A wolf wouldn't want to be in your room," said Papa.

"He wouldn't?" asked Rose.

"No," said Papa. "In his warm, furry coat,
he'd want to be outside playing with his friends,
under the stars."

Rose thought about that.

"If a wolf came into my room," she said,
"his claws might get caught in the carpeting."

"He might be afraid when you play with your noisy pop-up buzzer game first thing in the morning," said Papa.

"If we were having pizza for lunch," said Rose, "he'd like that."

"But he'd have to eat his vegetables if he wanted dessert," said Papa.

"And then he'd have to take a nap," said Rose.

"He'd probably want to," said Papa, "to get a cookie at snack time."

"Yes," said Rose. "But then he might get
his nose stuck in my cookie jar."
"Ouch!" said Papa.

22

"We could do finger painting all afternoon," said Rose.

"Paw painting," said Papa.

"Then we'd have to take a bath," said Rose,
"but he wouldn't like getting his hair washed . . .

or having it brushed to get out all the tangles."

"He probably wouldn't like having his nails trimmed, either," said Papa.

26

"Or brushing his teeth," said Rose.

28

"Then it would be bedtime," said Papa.

"Yes," said Rose. "I'd tell him, 'Put on your pajamas if you want to hear a bedtime story.'"

29

"Would he want a bedtime story?" asked Papa.

"No," said Rose.

"Right," said Papa, tucking Rose into bed. "A wolf wouldn't care about bedtime stories."

"I know what the big, scary wolf would care about," whispered Rose.

"What?" asked Papa.

"Playing outside with his friends, under the
stars," said Rose, closing her eyes.